Many Blessings
Marilyn
(the author of this book)

For baby Bryus Kiewing
with Gods Blessings!
Love Cindy Wollengien

# PRAYERS of THANKS and

# WONDER for CHILDREN

by
Marilyn Harkrider

illustrated by
Jerry Vineyard

For my grandfather, Dr. Peter H. Pleune, a pastor and man of God all of his life. A tall man, my grandfather awed the little ones of his congregation as he stood in his doctoral robes behind the pulpit, but his true stature was shown to them when he came down from the pulpit each Sunday for his children's sermon. After the small talk, and before we left the sanctuary he listened to our questions. No question was "stupid" or too small. As with the adults in the church he did not dictate faith, he led all to it. He understood "Faith beyond all understanding."

# INTRODUCTION

These small prayers are from a child's point of view, but with thoughts for adults to ponder, also. Non-denominational and universal in scope these prayers of wonder and thanks can spark discussions between children and the adults in their lives as to who God is and how He is seen in the child's family's beliefs.

Dear God,

Thank You for my toys.

They give me joy and I can make a joyful noise with them.

They help me explore my world.

Amen

Dear God,

Thank You for trees.

I can climb them.

I can see my world when I am up in them.

They are homes for birds.

Thank You, God, for trees.

Amen

Thank You, God, for rabbits.

They hop like I do, and they are cute.

You made them cute to enjoy when I see one in the grass.

Amen

Thank You, God, for crayons.

I can match the bright colors You made
for me to see.

Sometimes I draw something, and
sometimes

I just scribble, but I can have fun seeing
the rainbow colors on my page.

Amen

Thank You, God for ants in the ground.

They are fun to watch.

Do people look like that to You?

You are so big. Are we so small to You?

I like it when people work together like ants.

Amen

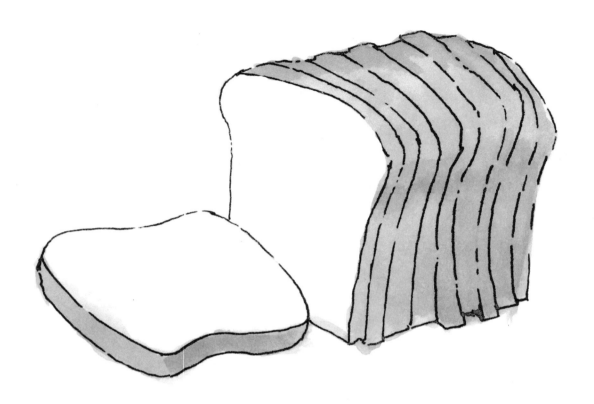

Thank You, God, for bread. It is great for a sandwich.

The slices keep the sticky filling from getting on my fingers.

What does "Man does not live by bread alone" mean?

Do I have to eat my vegetables too?

Amen

6

Thank You for my pets, God.

They give me love.

They understand and talk quietly to me.

They are warm and cuddly.

You must have a special place in Your heart for animals.

They do Your work without complaining.

Could You train them to make my bed?

Amen

Thank You, God, for doors.

I like to jump out and go "Boo" from behind them.

They keep my toys safe when I am away from home.

They make a great bang when I close them hard. I bet You can hear that.

I am not as loud as a banging door and You hear me.

Amen

Thank You, God, for juice and milk.

They taste good.

They really make a mess when my glass is spilled.

I don't think it is awful when it happens. It is interesting.

Did You spill Your milk when You made the clouds?

Amen

God, thank You for my body.

I love to feel my feet walk and my hands clap and my tummy gurgle.

Did it take You a long time to think up how we were going to be made?

You did a good job.

Amen

Dear God, I don't have a question. I will figure this one out all by myself.

You know when a person wants to get rid of something they will sometimes say they are going to cross it out?

Well, Jesus crossed out our sins. So I think He got rid of them.

I hope You don't get tired of my questions like some adults do sometimes.

That's why I am not asking You this one.

I will just think about what it means to me.

Amen

Dear God, why did You make poison ivy?

It doesn't do anybody any good. Sometimes I can't figure You out.

Please help my poison ivy stop itching.

If You have ever had poison ivy You will know what I mean.

Oh, I forgot You don't have a body. Do you?

You are lucky. You can't get itchy if You have no body.

Amen

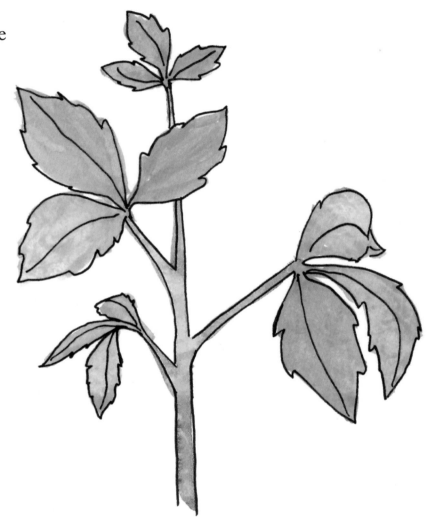

God, thank You for lights.

I am not as afraid when they are on. If You are the light of the world

should I be less afraid because You are on? I think so.

Amen

Thank You, God, for my friends.

I share with them. Sharing is good. It makes me feel together with others.

Friends make me laugh, but sometimes they are mean.

I guess I have to work that out with them if they are not always nice.

Why are people mean sometimes?

Thank You for my friends even when I am mad at them.

Amen

Dear God, how can hurt be good?

I got a shot today. It hurt.

That was bad, but it was supposed to be good for me.

Is it the same when I get spanked?

I don't know if I want to say, thank You, for hurt.

Amen

Chairs are nice. Thank You, God.

I run around a lot and don't use them much, but when I do I am comfy.

I hear stories in them too.

If my soul rests do I sit down on You?

Amen

Thank You, God, for me.

I love me.

I am beautifully made by You.

You see I'm wonderful.

Amen

Thank You, God for stars.

They remind me of fireflies, but Mommy says they stay on all the time.

Are they the night lights in Your many mansions?

Mommy says Your creation is very big and that I cannot see all of it.

I don't know if I understand that. I understand big buildings.

If I can't see all of Your universe how do I know it is there?

Is that faith beyond all understanding?

Thank you for stars. They really keep me wondering.

Amen

Dear God, our bathtub ran over the other day. Mommy was upset.

Did Your bathtub overflow when Noah built his ark? Daddy said You promised not to do that again. I guess You got things fixed. We didn't get a rainbow after our flood. All we got was soggy carpet.

But when the bathtub is acting right, I love to play in the water. I feel so good and clean when I get out. My body is happy.

Is that what bathtism is? A person cleans their inside feelings, and they are happy. I think it is.

Some people do not do that, but they believe in You. I do not think they are dirty though.

Thank You God for bathtubs and baths.

Amen

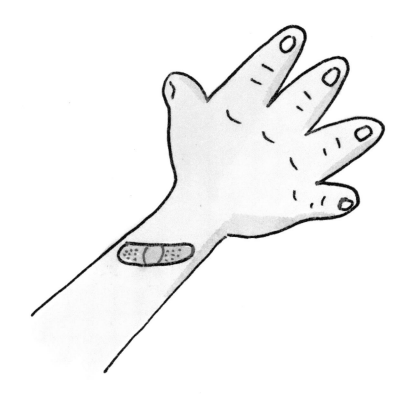

Thank You, God, for band aids.

They help when I get a cut.

I don't feel so bad after a kiss and a band aid.

I think prayers are like band aids and kisses.

They help a person heal inside.

Amen

Dear God,

Thank You for super heroes.
They are very strong and
powerful, and they fight evil.
I like the way they fight the bad
guys and always win.

I wish that I could be a super hero.
I pretend, but I am just me. Maybe
being the best I can be makes me a
super hero.

I think everyone can do great
things if they try, but they can't
fly, or see through a building.

I know You are the Super Hero
of all super heroes.

You are strong and You fight evil too.

Thank You for protecting me.

Amen

Thank You for music, God.

It makes me feel happy. Music is so beautiful. I love to hear it and move to it.

I love to sing in church.

I cannot sing like the music, but I try.

A lady goes to our church who cannot sing. She tries to sing the hymns anyway.

Is that what You mean by making a joyful noise? She is a nice lady. I am glad she is joyful.

I hope that we do not hurt your ears. Do you have ears?

I asked Daddy if You could put big speakers in the sky and play pretty music.

He said if that happened we could not hear the beautiful music of nature.

I think he is right.

People should make their own music.

Thank You for music.

Amen

Hummingbirds are so little, and they flit around.

My Mommy says You take care of even the birds.

I am not a bird, but I am little, and I sometimes flit around.

Hummingbirds remind me that You care for even the smallest animals; even me.

Thank You for noticing me too.

Amen

Thank You for my food each day, God.

I like apples. Do You like apples?

I guess You do; You made them.

Do You eat?

Thank You for apples and I guess onions.

I do not like onions too much. Is that alright?

Is that what free will is?

Amen

God, do You like glue?

I do. It sticks things together when I make something with paper.

My Mommy says love is like glue. It sticks things together.

Thank You for glue and love.

Amen

God, I am not sure I want to grow up. Today is my birthday. I like my life.

Some of my friends think it would be wonderful to be big.

Why do I want to stay small? Big people protect me when I am small.

Will You protect me when I am big? I guess so.

Everyone is Your child.

OK, Thank You for birthdays.

Amen

Daddy was talking about the man who owns the company he works for.

That man makes all the big decisions.

Daddy says it is sometimes lonely at the top.

Are You lonely? I hope not.

You are the head of everything.

I will try to make You not lonely. I will talk to You every day.

Thank You for being in charge of all things.

Amen

Thank You, for glasses, God.

My aunt wears them and she sees better.

My uncle says some people cannot see clearly even with their glasses on.

What does that mean?

I cannot see You, but I know You are there.

Sometimes I am confused.

I know You will be there to help me straighten things out.

Amen

Thank You, God, for all the colors of the world.

They are beautiful.

I am glad the sky is blue and the grass and trees are green.

That is peaceful to look at all day.

Red and orange wouldn't be good, for all day, I don't think, but I like those colors in sunrises and sunsets.

You had a good plan.

Amen

Thank You God for bees.
I know they sting, but
my teacher says they are
important for food.

They do a thing called
pollination that makes flowers
produce fruit and other things.

They are small, but important
to You. I am small and
important to You too, like the
bees.

I want to do something
important for You.

Amen

Thank You for police. Mommy says some people blame them when bad things happen, but they try to keep us safe.

Most police are good people who work hard for us.

My aunt blamed You for a long time because she lost her sight. Is that fair? I don't think so.

My grandmother says bad things just happen sometimes.

My aunt finally got over being mad at You. I am glad.

I think police would be glad if people weren't mad at them.

Could You help people not be mad at each other?

Amen

Thank You, God, for pictures.

They are nice because I can remember what my Grand Mommy and Granddaddy look like. They live far away.

I can remember what places I had fun visiting looked like too. I like to remember the park and the beach.

You don't need pictures, I guess. You see everything all the time.

I need pictures, and if I were You, I would not know where to look first.

Thank You for pictures.

Amen

Ice cream is yummy. It makes me happy. That is what it does.

Are some things here just to make us happy? I think so.

Ice cream is one of the best. If I get it in a bowl I want to lick the bowl to get the last drop.

Mommy says that is not polite, but it is hard not to.

Is that temptation?

I just love ice cream, but I will try not to lick the bowl.

Amen

Thank You, God, for seashells.
They are so pretty. I love to find them in the beach.

Mommy says that animals used to live inside.

I heard my grandfather say some people make shells around themselves.

What does that mean?

Do people get hard? I will think about that.

Thank You for shells.

Amen

Thank You for thunder, God.

My cousin is afraid of it, but I think it sounds powerful like You.

Are You just trying to say "Here I am"?

If You have such a loud voice why can't some people hear You?

I wish You could talk to me in words sometimes. I will still listen when it rains.

Amen

35

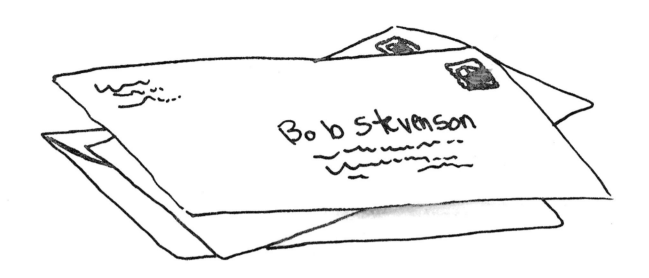

I love mail. Thank You, God for mail.

I get cards and letters from people I love, and that makes me happy.

Do You send mail?

I know You send many messages for people so they can know You, but have You ever written a letter?

Thank You for the mail I get, and thank You for Your messages of love.

Amen

Dear God, thank You for TV and computers.
I can only have a little "screen time" a day, but I see such wonderful things… different places, animals, plants, numbers, and I guess that is why I wonder about things.

There is so much in the world I do not know. I do know You are there.
My teacher says that is faith, and a person cannot see faith.
Maybe TV and computers are a way to know You though.
I can see so much of what You make.

Amen

Phones ring and interrupt dinner, but thank You for them anyway.

I can talk to my grandparents and cousins who do not live near me.

My aunt says we can stay connected when we talk on the phone.

I like to be connected.

I wish I could call You.

I do not think You have a phone number.

I guess I will just have to talk to You in my prayers.

Amen

Thank You, God, for really smart people. I know everyone is equal in Your eyes, and even I know people have many different wonderful talents to share.

But, everyone knows that some people are smarter than others.

One of my friends is really smart. He can think of things I cannot. Maybe he will grow up to help invent something or find a cure for a disease. Maybe he will run a business really well.

We all can help each other, but I think You put smart people here for making a really big difference in the world for many, many people.

Thank You for them. Help other people not to be jealous.

Help me do my best when I grow up.

Daddy says it is living up to my potential.
Thank You for giving me my potential.

Amen

Sleep is something I do not want to do sometimes, God.

I do not want to go to bed. I am too busy exploring.

My parents say I need to grow, and let my brain rest.

Sometimes when I cannot sleep I think about a lot of things.
I think about You too.

My grandfather says You do not sleep. Don't You get tired?

He says You are constantly watching over us. That is a big job. I would
get tired. Every living thing sleeps, so I guess I am supposed to too.

Thank You for sleep, but could You get my parents to make my
bedtime a little later?

Mommy says You can do anything. Does it work that way?

Amen

Dear God, thank You for the sun, the rain, the snow and all that weather stuff.

I do get upset when it rains sometimes. I can't go outside to play. I wish it would just rain when I am asleep. My friends feel that way too.

But, I guess I would not have puddles to jump in afterwards.

I guess rain isn't so bad.

It makes the vegetable garden grow, and I like the tomatoes.
I love the flowers too.

Thank you for all the weather.

One question; why are there hurricanes? They are not good for anything.

Amen

Thank you for pickles, God.

There are all different kinds of pickles, but I like the dill ones.

My cousin likes sweet pickles.

Why do people have different likes in pickles?
I guess because no one is the same.

Maybe if everyone liked dill pickles my mom would have a hard time buying them at the store. They would be gone.

Thank you for dill pickles and making everyone different.

Amen

Thank You for You, but what do I call You?

You have more than one name. They are hard to pronounce, Jehovah, Yahweh, and now my new friend says he calls You Allah.

I have many names. My mom calls me "Hon," my grandmother calls me "Sweetie," my dad "Dear Child" when they do not use what my friends call me.

I even have three names I was given when I was born. I answer to them all.

Do You? Do You have a favorite name? Did You pick it out?

If I made up a name would You know I was talking to You?

What if I called You Fred? Would You mind? It would be easier to pronounce than the others.

God isn't hard though, so I guess I will just call You that.

Good night God. I love You.

Amen

# Dear God, Thank You for...

*This page is to record a child's own prayers of wonder and thanks.*

44

# Dear God, Thank You for...

*This page is to record a child's own prayers of wonder and thanks.*

45

# Author's Previous Books...

## Santa, Is it Really You?

If you have ever wondered why there are so many men dressed up like Santa in stores and malls, then you have found your explanation in this story.

It all began long ago with a discussion between Mrs. Claus and Santa and a surprise meeting with a little boy named Ben. As you magically travel through the years with Santa, you will find the answer to the question you will never have to ask again.

This is a story that is sure to become a family favorite and tradition during the Christmas season. The exquisite illustrations will make the beautiful tale come alive for young and old alike. Merry Christmas!

## Mademoiselle Meringue Bayou Baby

A fluffy kitten is born into the Cajun world of the Louisiana bayou. As she grows up with her two brothers File and Bourg, they experience their heritage in their many adventures. Their friend Jacques Uar accompanies them as they romp through the bayou, experience the joys of Thanksgiving Cajun style, receive presents from Papa Noel at Christmas, and celebrate Mardi Gras in the bayou. Some of their adventures take them to a Hoodoo queen, scare them with the "cocodries" and make them fight for their blackberry patch.

Using authentic background, history, and vocabulary of the Cajun area of southern Louisiana, the book gives the reader a sense of being in that area and knowing the tradition as a participant. The Cajun vocabulary is defined after each word used, and a glossary is available for reference.

Entertaining, fun, and educational, Mademoiselle Meringue Bayou Baby is a view of the world from a growing kitten's eyes, but the insights she acquires are wonderfully human.

## Mademoiselle Meringue

A kitten born in the bayou, Mademoiselle Meringue, has grown up and found a home in New Orleans Louisiana. Her adventures are as varied as the city itself, and as the reader sees the city through the perspective of this feline and her friends they absorb much of the rich history of the "Big Easy" as well. With a reference and glossary page included the reader experiences the educational aspect of the book in a more traditional way, also.

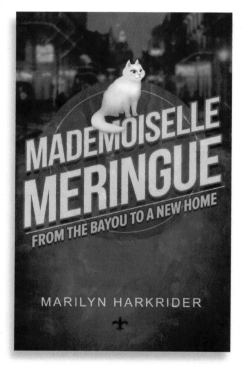

Meringue may be older, but the scrapes and adventures are no less thrilling than those of her kitten hood. Join the fun, and "let the good times roll."

**Tub Teaching for Tots**

This science teacher approved book of learning experiences for young children is a fun way for a child to be exposed to many simple scientific principles.

While having fun in the tub these simple and inexpensive experiences are created with things found in your home, and serve as not only building blocks for later learning, but are fun. They provide a unique experience, which allows the child and the grown-up a platform for sharing ideas both educational and personal when applied to the experiences they have shared together. Mastery of the concepts is not expected, but as the fun continues with repeated and new "lessons" the ideas will form in the reservoir of the child's knowledge.

Bonding with fun; With no mess to clean up;
What could be better!?

## Snore Me Safe, Daddy

What was that? Was it a witch's fingers scratching the window? Was it a ghost scraping its chains? Was it a giant asking his name? And what about the noises coming from inside?

A new house, strange sounds outside his window and Sam's imagination is running wild. His trusted bear, Tedders, is not helping his fears. What will make those fears go away? How will he ever get any sleep? The solution is not far away. But, Sam will need some help finding out what it is.

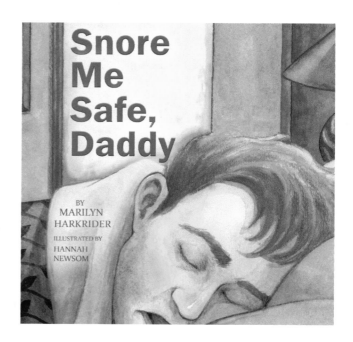

*Books to come:*

**Wonderful World of Words**

A Series of books aimed at young children, but relevant to all, this series teaches about English and language in a humorous and interesting way. The first two books in the series will be available in early 2016.

**– Lollipops and Latin Roots – A Sweet Discovery 1**

English, Spanish, French and other languages have Latin roots as the building blocks of many words. When learned these can increase the ease of word definition and language acquisition. They are gems forgotten. In the light-hearted and sometimes silly couplets of this book, rhyme, pictures and fun help the reader find a lifelong language tool in a fun way.

**– Lollipops and Latin Roots – A Sweet Discovery 2**

With the same approach as book one Discovery 2 uses two roots in a word rather than exploring one at a time. The reader not only has the fun discovering more roots, but begins to realize these really work together and are found all over English.

## Happy Christmas Merry Hanukah

While swinging at school these two little boys discover that they celebrate differently during the winter holiday break. In a light touch this story explores the sharing each does of the other's traditions and beliefs as they grow closer as friends. Beautifully illustrated these two related beliefs come alive in a warm way for children to understand as the story unfolds. Based on a true story.

## The Courageous Cuckoo

Trapped not only in his clock, but in his own shyness, this little bird, Hans, must find the courage to leave the clock shop. Loved and encouraged by Mr. Strauss, the clock maker, Hans tries to find his future in the home of a nice family, but he cannot conquer his fears. Finally, something happens and his bravery allows him to fly to his future. Old world illustrations make this delightful tale even more enchanting.

CPSIA information can be obtained at www.ICGtesting.com
Printed in the USA
LVIW01n0742071016
507595LV00002B/4